PANTHEON

2

ISBN 0-9659576-0-8

T? L.

4

TABLE OF CONTENTS

PANTHEON

the First Panther Cycle: Out of the Night

BROODING EYES

felicity and cunning claws.
hunger in the hunter's jaws.
angel's heart and devil's prize.
the panther prowls with brooding eyes.
soulful eyes and soulless dreams.
maddened by the new will's screams.
mortal. and yet, set apart
by what is locked within her heart.

NIGHT STALKER

in the night.
in the jungle.
in the depths of sad despair.
there's a presence.
in the branches.
you can't see her. but she's there.
watching closely.
taking measure.
are you predator? are you prey?
and if either.
does she leave you?
does she seek to pounce and play?
and if neither.
does she linger?
and then fall. into your trap?
will the hunter.
be the hunted.
when she hears the steeljaw snap?
will she struggle?
or surrender?
will she know. you mean no harm?
understanding.
like the panther.
that this fire can be warm?
it is quiet.
in this jungle.
if you listen. with your soul.
and this silence.
calls the panther.
to protect it. and patrol.

APHRODITE'S FOUNTAIN

I drifted, in a skeptic's trance,
beyond the sphere where shadows dance
and lovers pray for second chance
to merge like spring-swift rivers.

and in the jungles of the night,
two eyes were there, in brooding bright,
reflecting from an inner light
a hunger and a feasting.

the panther came in graceful stalk
to the fountain where the ancients talk
of heroes who weep and victims who mock
the memory of their passions.

and in the branches overheard
there lay a sentinel in his bed,
a dragon gold with eyes of red,
enwrapped in ardored patience.

his wings unfurled and blocked the sky.
he flew to the cat, and for a moment I
feared for her death and knew not why
she did not flee in terror.

and then the wonder was enhanced
by these two beasts in courtier's dance.
they swirled as though by fate entranced
around the sacred fountain.

I did not watch, I did not see
if those two coupled 'neath the tree
that stands beyond the whispering sea
of pain and dreams and madness.

at length they lay, entwined and spent
and left me wondering what it meant
that they should care to be content,
this panther and her paramour.

strange beasts were they, and still they lay,
beneath that tree so far away,
next to the font where angels play.
and smile at their communion.

the Third Panther Cycle: the Rainbow

THE VIOLETS

a thousand dainty flowers, fragrant and sweet,
growing in a bed not given to recent gardener's care.
needing tending and words of encouragement.
the master's hand. the touch of one who cares
what may spring from the bidding loam from
which spring these sweet flowers. I nuzzle
this luxuriant bed of subtle fragrance and dream
of a dream of a dream of a dream of a dream.

the Fourth Panther Cycle: I Dreamed a Dream

SEVENTH MONTH

I lay with you, my arms entwined about your quiet form,
my hands softly and reverently feeling the curve
of the chamber wherein lays the labor of our love.
beautiful angel, forged of our passions, summoned
by love, she rests and awaits her coming life.
and our coming joy at her birth. I am at peace
with this. filled with joy that she is ours and
will live as a glorious testament to our love and hope.
and I feel her stir within you. and I weep.

WHEN FIRST I CHANCED

when first I chanced to hear your voice
my heart stopped.
not for want of death, but because
nothing can change
in the space between beats of your heart.
and I wanted you
to forever speak my name. with reverence
and honest love.

when first I chanced to look into your eyes
burnt gold honey
in colour. my breath caught. the air
was no longer needed
to sustain my life. for in your eyes
my world held, strung
on wires of platinum and steel and dreams.
and honest love.

when first I chanced to touch your flesh
my life ended.
and began again. the minuet of life paused
and then continued.
and I was caught in the dance. intoxicated
by your warm hand.
by the sweet message in your smile. bold
with honest love.

when first I chanced to lay with you
the angels wept.
knowing what was in my heart, how could
they but regret
never knowing what passes between two lovers
caught in the sphere
where ends all reality and the truth is pure as
any sacrament.

when first I chanced to speak of love
you smiled at me.
and touched me with a hand that stole
my life. and spoke
with a voice that stopped my heart.
and looked on me
with eyes that caught my breath. and I knew.
I knew. I know.

4 A.M.

as you lay beside me in sleep I place my ear, gently
so as not to awaken you, against your flesh and listen
to the steady beat of your heart and the gentle flow
of the night air in and out of your lungs. and I weep.
for I love you so much. and your peace is beautiful.

the Ninth Panther Cycle: A Slice of Heaven

INFLUENCES

small hands. big heart. sweet smile. your part
in my life is undefined, but monumental.
you have refined and redefined my dreams, central
to the paths I will choose. win or lose, my heart
is yours. feed upon it if the need is great, share
with it if the feeling is upon you, but never doubt
my sincerity and commitment. my soul pours out
in pools of holy water to wash away your cares.

THE PENETRATING ROSE

the focus shifts to your hand. your soft hand. the hand
that brushes aside my hair to gaze into my eyes when
that is all we dare do for fear of showing the cards
of our hearts to the riverboat gamblers who charge
and bluff and cheat their ways across this game. with
firm and cautious resolve, you guide the penetrating rose
to its vase. or perhaps, to a new bed, rich and nurturing.
where it will take root. and grow strong as an expression
of passion and love. I stare deeply into your burnt honey
eyes and see the fire in them, as parts the impediments
to the penetrating rose. I see your eyes. I feel your eyes
locked into mine, sending fire and pleasure like some
great spiritual semaphore. a single sound escapes your lips.
and the penetrating rose slides softly into place. and
you brush aside my hair again, with the soft hand that
guided the flower to its new home. where it takes root.
and blossoms as your eyes, hand, heart and flesh desire.

SONNET: THE JOURNEY

I have stood at the edge of eternity and watched the gravel
beneath my toes fall away into the endless void. down
into the abyss. for so long did I wander free and travel,
deemed mad by all who saw the decade's dance turn brown
the greenery of my youth. alone and arrogant, I traced
the line of a shining path of cunning calculations culled
from my perceptions of life and love and god. and faced
with mortality, I laughed a hearty roar. and when called
by fate to answer for my sins, I took my cross with grace
and peace, knowing that truth was a better companion
than anyone I'd ever known. until now. I turn my face
from the lonely wind and hold out my hand to ask you join
this lonely quest. alone no more, for I have found worth
in one who shares so much and I would share my time on Earth

RATIONALE

if sometimes I seem possessive
or suspicious, please forgive me.
it is no count against you. I live
for your love and through my eyes I see
no reason for one as wondrous
as you to love such as I am, all too
mortal. and sometimes, this marvelous
gift of your love, bestowed on me through
no worthiness of my own, makes me fear
that one day you will regain your reason
and see me for all my unworthiness, not near
to all you deserve. and in this season
of senses reawakened, you will depart
as you came, a luminous herald of joy
unasked. the gem of wonder within my heart
that grants me the most perfect peace any
man has ever known. my derelict heart bleeds
to think one day I'll be insufficient to your needs.

PANTHER EYES

burnt honey eyes, rich and rapturous.
a hunter's hunger made perilous.
eyes aglow with passion and delight.
smile affixed in soul's coherent light.
framed in dark illusions of the night.
burnt honey eyes, rich and rapturous.
the moment the fire consumes us.
I cannot look away, flesh made porous.
eyes aglow with passion and delight.
later, alone in the swirl of bright
memories, I see your smile, so right.
burnt honey eyes, rich and rapturous.
sitting in a crowd of friends, to us
there are more than words connecting us.
eyes aglow with passion and delight.
all I need is your glance to feel thrust
into the chaos of passionlight.
burnt honey eyes, rich and rapturous.
eyes aglow with passion and delight.

UNION

do you really want to love me?
I am unworthy so often, self-absorbed
and given to the excess of ego of my
gender and my art. I will never see
a mirror without my demons, barbed
fangs and nails clinging tightly. why
you would want this tortured man
is a puzzle to me. but you give me
love and serenity. a home for this
vagabond heart. a holy band can
bind us, but no tighter than I wish
to be at one with you in an eternal kiss.

the Eighteenth Panther Cycle: Unborn Memories,
Poetry Written by our Unborn Children

THE CONFESSION

long before I was born, a shy phrase
spoken. almost silent, a footnote
to a long and rambling letter of a praise
for a friend found dear. a dust mote
of affection, expressed and found fecund.
a fertile thought planted in a field
of willing embracement. love beckoned
in a daring slight of memory, healed.

the Nineteenth Panther Cycle: Seven Wonders

THE STATUE OF ZEUS
BY PHIDIAS AT OLYMPIA

I am glad we do not live in the time of the ancient Gods,
for Zeus was known for his knack for spying the most
beautiful and comely of women, and I would not like to
have to go toe to toe with the King of the Gods, as he
would, undoubtedly, kick my ass from here to kingdom
come, unless the other Gods said "Look, big guy, they
are in love...can't you cut him some slack?", and then
the ambrosia would almost certainly hit the fan.

THE ROSE

I remember that night
a thousand lifetimes ago
when we lay, joined by the light
of our passions, the penetrating rose
serving as bridge and conduit
for our hungers. our needs.
our open and honest love through it
feeding our memory. planting seeds
of revelation and obscurement
of issues we did not wish to embrace.
the petals, their colour and scent
intoxicating us. a singular vase.

SOULWIND

no leaf is stirred.
none. the dark
serenity is total
and focused.

you have tapped
into the sonic boom
of my heart in moments
captured in your world.

I have seen our future
in the golds of a simple
sky, held transfixed by
a prophetic constellation.

and when it roars, it
is deafening to all
but your voice. my choice
is made. and I will fly.

my wings are new,
but built from an ancient
design left ravaged on a
distant hill in fear and pain.

and I will not return.
never. to this graveyard
of my immortal soul. feral
hearts sing songs of victory.

CASSIOPEIA

the darkness of your myth will live in soulful eyes
reflecting proud lineage and a heritage of passion.
carry yourself proudly, my child, and know that wise
men and women do not mock the gods of creation
without a champion at hand. and I stand ready,
until Perseus makes his entrance in the third act,
to fill that role, as is my purpose and intent. steady
to the purpose of your conception against reasons packed.

the Twenty-Fourth Panther Cycle: inevitability

PANTHERS AND POETS

Panthers and poets. I did not design the tapestries.
but there they are, spread before me in red and gold
and green and a fiery black brought from distant galaxies.
I would ride to them with you, for I knew when bold
I quenched my thirst for holy communion in your kiss
that this is where God meant me to be. this mislaid
destiny. I will find my path, picking among the ruins
of those who can not, will not, dare not bless this parade
of the life artists within us. but it is truth of iron
and living silver, and just this once I will drink wines
the path ordained. the ennobling cutting of my open
heart will bring me down to my knees a thousand times
for crimes imagined, but without your love I well
cannot live. and I will not. even if shackled in Hell.

NUCLEAR INFERNO

You can never reach breakeven, they say,
the fires will fall away before you get
the power to a level required for fusion.
But the secret is not in the converging
lasers or the Maglich toroids, but the fuel.

Nothing achieves the flashpoint if the way
you seek the fire is in putting in sweat
for the flaws in the hydrogen cores. When
you find the signature spectrum emerging
from the purest tritium, the reaction will rule.

THE FIRES OF LOVE

I didn't come this way on purpose. But here
I have to admit I am frighteningly comfortable.
We fit. If God carved me a merging mate, surely
he gave her soulful burnt honey eyes and a feral
panther's dance. A simple stance from chance
revealed me in want of this fractured fragment
of my spirit's hologram to dispel the haze
of confusion. If arriving late to the banquet
thrown in my honor is sin, then I am guilty.
Let the fires be lit and the flames point
the way, let every woman or man have a right
to their panther. Let the dreams be illuminated
with the fated touch of lovers cut of single
cloth but obscured by fate or folly long past.
Stand on the parapets of the keep and watch
the firewinds of love sweep the valley free
of the debris of sad night songs. Strong
is the power of love. Made in the image of
God, we seek the divine spark that lights the
taper, the taper of hope that catches the flame
to set the blazing hearts to burn as they race
towards conflagration. And, when the light
is made coherent in the poets dreams and
themes, and the fuel is pure, the fusion
is achieved and we build to the fire of love.

EMERALD

like that dress of legend. I see you in it
(when my fantasies are clothed), lovely
and elegant. legs for days and the sweet
beauty you possess focused by the way
your eyes catch the green fire. my desire
was held at bay, there with everyone around,
but I was taken with your charms and proud
that every man took at least a moment to steal
a lupine glance at you. and wanting to dance
with you. as I would, later. with the
emerald cloth set aside, but in my heart.

POETRY

you have the muse.
oh, sometimes you doubt it,
but when the coffee house
patrons stop stirring their
overpriced
decaf
to catch the turn
of a phrase you constructed
and brought to me like a
child
showing off a
handmade kite,
you must know
better. I have
learned from you
and your work
stands on
its own pentameters.

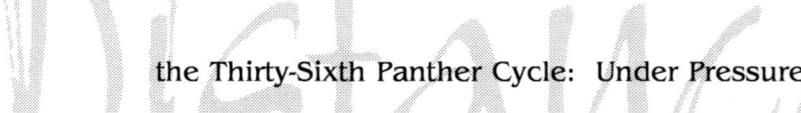

the Thirty-Sixth Panther Cycle: Under Pressure

DISTANCE AND DANCES

I cannot kiss you goodnight tonight.
I cannot hold you close and tightly
meld my sleeping breath with yours
as we dream together, visions pure
and plutonic. memories we share
in a future life, time that will bear
down on us like a welcome train
carrying us on a honeymoon in Spain.

the Forty-first Panther Cycle: Reweaving the Tapestries

PULSE POINT

her heart is all that beats within me.
and when the pulse points are faint,
I paint my face ashen and withered.
the source of all the greatest joy
receding in the veins of time. many
are my sins, and I am no mortal saint,
but God has blessed me, sadness cured
and hope made manifest for eternity.

SERENITY

and when I am tired.
and uninspired
to live my life beyond
the morning, dawn
holding terrors dreamed
in a tortured scream
into a pillow, I recall
the words so small
they fill the universe
and lift the curse
of fear from my madness.
and I am blessed
by your love. and raised
for the coming days.

the Forty-Third Panther Cycle: actions of love

WALKING TOGETHER

I will never be alone. for in my heart I carry
the memories and majesty of you. I'll marry
myself to what the future should have been
and live with the repercussions of once again
dreaming beyond my means. by my side
is but a phantom, a zujembie bride
cut of the pride I felt in your elevation
of me to the plateau where, in celebration
of life and love, sadness and joy, panthers play
their games of life art and chase pain away.

IN TARNISHED MEMORY

in tarnished memories made mockery
by our weakness, left on the nightstand
like a wilting rose. discarded and unregarded
as we move to other sport, we contort
our dreams to match our paths and laugh
with self-deprecating humour at the rumours
we can validate only in silence. the violence
of time, worked on us all. the seconds ticking
and the phone ringing a rude song, bringing
unknown answers to dancers too far apart
to ever touch again. and, as such, in pain.

THE SONG OF THE PANTHER

a voice like a haven from death,
breath passed through a soul
dancing in pain, in vain to escape
the rape of time. the field
of orchids is not yet in season
for the roses are still
omnipresent and pleasant
enough. petals testing the
mettles of us all. a choice to
voice sorrow and a curious
question that belies resolve.
to solve the riddle
of the sphinx I met
in a quiet restaurant
when I touched the face
of God.

the Forty-Eighth Panther Cycle: Dreams of Iron
and Sapphire

HEARTBEAT

one day
I will lay my head again
again your soft back
and listen to the reassurance
of your heart,
beating out a rhythm
clocked by God
to let me live
and love at a level
unimagined before
you moved my hair
with your hands
and made me promise
names to our future children.

WINGS OF A BLACK DOVE

the nemicorn came to me
in a new form. warm with
promise and power, a flower
of black silk. milk sipped
greedily from nursing breasts
to test the passion that fashions
a monument immortal, but feeble
in the face of a black lace fan
of wings rising from the bold
shoulders of a panther transcending
the ground, ascending to bound
with the dragons in the skies
where dies no legend.

THE COOKIE JAR

it did not break.
I did not know it could take
a fall from so great a height.
grand is my delight
knowing that the ceramic
skin over this romantic
soul is more resilient
than first thought. spent
crumbs spicing the air
whenever the lid is opened.
but sometimes we pretend
not to care what is inside
out of hunger and the pride
born of fear. fear the oatmeal
raisin prayers will not find real
satience in the jar. and so
we will starve. alone with no
hope. just memories of a jar.
kept empty. kept far.

THE WELL AT KYRIENAR

the dry well. ever dry of water.
but not of joy. or purpose.
made as a monument to a daughter
who chased the winged faeries
in the clearing, nearing the curve
of the songs at their apogee.
if you stand at the rim and sing
the ancient songs, you will hear
more than your voice return.
for Cassiopeia's faeries dwell
in the dark when she is away,
and play mumble-the-peg
with splinters of sapphire
until she gets home from school.

THE CASTLE

she dwelled there for a season.
and, finding it fit, yet another.
but soon she wearied and went
on. and the Castle, just at the edge
of the land of the Gods, fell into
sad disrepair. but, when she had
grown her black lace wings and
strength and reason and the urge
to build on things with some
resonance became a new thread,
she had it refurbished. and she
would daily wave from the highest
tower to the herb merchants
in her courtyard and go down
to taste the essences of whim.

the Fifty-Third Panther Cycle: Cassiopeia's Garden

WILDFLOWERS

fistfuls of colour
to give to my mother.
to show her I love her.

ELOQUENCE

I asked for love and it was granted,
handed me like a mercury-triggered
thermonuclear device. with a wink
and a smile God said it was mine
to deal with as best I could. Oh, good.
just what I need...riding close enough
to the edge I can feel the gravel beneath
my wheels in that childhood nightmare.
waiting for the doors to open and see
what makes me scream. not a dream.
but I rule my heart, or so the illusion
goes. I chose to harness the team
of horses of greatest power and trust
one day I might control them. and for
a thousand reasons they lead me down
a road I can think of a thousand reasons
I should not travel. my sanity unravels
and I am left to tie the last sweater
thread off to the pillars of the temple
of Aphrodite, in hopes that, in this
world of honest ignorance, there is truth
left in my left boot, to be poured out
like water after a walk in the puddles
left by a rain that won't be back until
a season on a calendar I do not have.

like a cyclone dancing in the fields
and all I can do is hope that the compass
points this way when it finally makes
its cut. for when all is said and done
I am tired of being a scarecrow
in the fields of love and devotion.
not so tired to quit, for I am made
of sterner stuff than that, I will let
my arms wither and drop before
I turn away from my heart's duty.
and I will let the skysharks pluck out
my eyes and tear the straw that once,
above the busy streets in the apple
orchard, was not straw, but iron.

the Fifty-Fifth Panther Cycle: an afternoon in
the company of a sand dragon

IIII.

I would like one day, my sandy friend,
to bring my children here to meet you.
perhaps by then your wings will have
sprouted, I have never doubted but that
you are a sand dragon, and it is only
fitting you meet my children. sitting
as the sun slides on its invisible rail
across the sky of impossible blue, we
will talk of dreams you are feeding me.
I see it in your eyes, do not deny it.
it was you who called me here, remember
how you stole my sleep? and now
I share my water, poured out to
give you precious moisture, while you
teach me introspection and courage,
two gifts I had lost, with my life,
to the winds of fear and separation.
no hesitation, had I it all to do
again, the only change I would make
would be in not coming to her side the
moment I saw she was sad. months
lost, maybe the path. and with no
backup for my seed, the quiet fear
that one day, the dreams will be ended
like a chandelier, cut suspended
to crash into my heart and give her
reason to seek another.

VII.

The sand beneath my shoes
makes noises louder than
the wind in the arms
of the succulents surrounding
me with their prickly arms.
and I am not retreating,
but returning to my world.
stronger and surer. the truth
of the sand dragon etched
in my soul. survival. and
simple questions best answered
one word at a time. and only
when the water is still wet, and
not bound in clouds held beyond
our reach. I will capture clouds
for you, and make the rain,
that you may dance with me
and the sand dragons. and the
children that we love. all the
children, that we love.

THE TOWER

I rode into hell, once. dark corridors painted white
to hide the festering sorrows I had to face. to race
the red drops of tears leavened with pain. now I find
I must dismount and climb the dizzying rails that circle
to a sky I never met before. a war I never wanted. haunted
by truths too bitter and brittle to smile upon me, free
to wreak havoc like hounds let to run in the woods
where the panther sleeps. where the panther creeps.
and where I will be, once the tower falls beneath my siege.

the Fifty-Eighth Panther Cycle: the deathless cycle

LISTENING WITH YOUR HEART

sometimes words are never spoken.
but they are meant. bent tokens
and fallen totems. the calling diadems
that crown the regents of our champions.
and on beyond our accepted limitations
is the truth and we must merely wait until
the tree bends in the winds of time, then
reach for it. and pray our fingers still
have the strength to seize. I do not know
what comes, but if it pleases you, I will
endorse it and dance at the wedding
of the woman I love. even if it is not mine.

41

the Sixtieth Panther Cycle: hours of the day

TWILIGHT

she wrote a poem, once.
beautiful and perfect, as she is...
a laugh within a tear within a dream
within a fantasy resplendent. dependent
on my arc. and so I launched my soul
like a ballistae bullet, and stayed where
I landed, deep in a jungle I will always
stay in. even when driven to the edge.
I will travel in the company of lesser beasts
and drink from streams where the waters
are quenching, but not sweet. beat the bushes
to flush quarry to kill wit verbal sling, sing
songs that echo in the valleys beyond Lur.
and watch my panther dancing on the beach.

the Sixty-First Panther Cycle: seven wishes

LUNCH

to talk over a salad and mugs of tea. like in that
restaurant in Fairfax, or the cafe in Little Italy
where the service was so poor, but it didn't seem
to matter so much as long you wore your suede
skirt and there was a flower shop down the street
where I could buy roses of intention. lingering
of mouthfuls of food and eyes full of love and dreams.

YOUR JOY

my grandson climbed into my lap and held out a book
to me. weathered with age, each page burned into my
memory like an immutable brand. he asked me who the
pretty lady was, whose picture marked the frontispiece.
I blinked back a few tears, shed a lifetime ago on a
battlefield where I was too busy agonizing over my role
in the conflict to take the point, as was my purpose.
I told him that she was just a dream I once met and
made happy for a season. then I sent him to play.

the Sixty-Third Panther Cycle: the wind in the desert

THE WIND AT NIGHT

the sweat of the day is gone.
on beyond the howling in the rocks
where a thousand years ago a priest danced
prayers unanswered by a god he imagined
gave a damn if he died of thirst, cursed
to haunt the valley for all eternity
until he learned the right steps.
and it cools me to sit here, in
the light of the stars, and dream
dreams just as damning.

THE COMMON TONGUE (SPEAK PLAINLY AND WITH TRUTH)

the orthography of poets
belongs in poetry.
not in words spoken
in pain or anger or fear
of losing something or someone
held so dear
that you feel death upon you.
that is a time for the babysteps
of simple words, where commonality
is more likely true. a basic
tongue where truths are not
garbled amid the noise of well meaning
friends who read letters like
Rorschach tests and listened that night
you raved until late, finding hate
in wounded love and bitter tears.

THAT HALF A HEART

I wonder if you still have it
buried in your breast
or is it on a shelf with
the shirt I gave you. the legacy
of searching love retired
having found the prize like
Moses at the Promised Land?
40 years in the desert to be told
that I will not pass.

are the daffodil cup and the
crazy ceramic wizard holding
nightly discussions?

or are they
with the boxed knick-knacks
held in impossibly tiny hands
as we made love.
in our minds.
in our souls.
in our dreams.
in our lives.
in our pasts.

THE TOUCH OF LIFE

your hands.
like God on the ceiling
of the Sistine chapel.
giving me life.
giving me hope.
redemption through grace
and the kiss of an angel
too long in a distant heaven.
too long between communion sips
from the lips of a feral woman
made legend
by my words,
but only speaking the truth
of what is inside.

THE RAIN WASHES AWAY ALL SORROWS

like sugar running in the flood
the blood
of martyrs is washed away
as we play
in the thunder
that punctuates your cries
as I punctuate your gentle body.
the lightning
arcs like your back as you attack
me over and over...swallowing
my seed, my soul, my life
in yours...
and the rain washes away all sorrows.

IF I AM TO LIVE WITHOUT FEAR

if I am to live without fear, then it must be in your arms.
for without them, the confusion and pain is a monument
to fallen hope. love will lay in ruins battered by the storms
of a thousand tropical summers. the coinage long spent
on tourist-trap trinkets unworthy of our dreams and touch.
buried in mountain snows to not melt in the history of man.
crushed beneath the tread of titans birthed with such
venom that they can only be the sons of a rage that began
deep within the despair of Sisyphus. we, as mortals, need
our Gods. for whether they are real, or myths, the legend
sustaining our souls. teaching us to live above our fears. read
the words you have summoned from a lover and a friend.
for when the next chronicles are taken, a panther and a poet
will live in these pages. for love. no fear. no regret.

PRIDE OF AUTHORSHIP

we pride ourselves on our creations.
and yet, our greatest work lays
obscured by all our work-room
clutter emotions. sawdust and
that lost hammer, thrown in a
corner, not out of disrespect,
but haste and auteur's passion.
this script is grander than any comedy,
this poem is sweeter than any cycle,
this evocation advertises the best
in woman and in man, better than any
brochure or slogan. we are the art
and will be judged one day in
the eyes and minds and hearts
of those who descend from our
actions and our fleshes, based
on our pride of authorship.

A PROPHET IN HIS CUPS

at the table in my prison in the city of Angels, I met
a man. a prophet in his cups. he regarded me with eyes
dull and deadly and told me my life. each word rang true
yet, through it all, I could not but hope he had you wrong.
long thoughts later, I cannot be sure. pure reason mocks
the ticking clock, the calculations are imprecise but elegant
if the intent is to tell the tale. the sale of indulgences
for a new religion. a smidgen of half-truths, sold to willing
convert, looking for her way out of her old faith. a wraith
that haunts a distant city. out of pity. out of shame.
calling a name she no longer publicly would use. to choose
to lose what little is left and fall into arms that might
redeem him at her expense. past tense promises never to see
the light of day and grey eyes meeting burnt honey shadows
of a gallows I already hung upon for far too long. the prophet
reminded me that only the brave deserve dessert with their humble pie.

THE FIRE THAT BURNS TWICE AS HOT

the fire that burns twice as hot
usually
(note the word)
usually
only burns for half the time.
but if you dare
to take it up a notch
to where gas becomes
nuclear plasma
and the oxidation
becomes fusion
it can last forever.
it is just few have
the courage
to burn so hot
that they blind
the world and
risk annihilating
the universe
with their glory.
for we are mortals and
immortality
frightens us.
so I will wait
in the torus
and see if you show.
for I saw the spark
in your eyes
as you raised your head
and dropped your guard
and held me
in a doorway
in New York.

NEAR MISS IN A KISS

you last words were
"don't worry. I love you."
and so I fell.
William Tell
me about the memories
that came for you at midnight.
laughing at your tears.
fears
made mortal.
a portal into hell
I took no pleasure
in taking.
forsaking an old oath
to hide in white washed walls
where no one called.
installed in the fool's palace.
a chalice of venom
offered and rejected.
bloody lips kiss concrete
and the feet
walk away.
walk away.
walk away.

the Eighty-Second Panther Cycle: definitions of love

BETWEEN TWO BODIES (A RESPONSE)

I am held to your orbit.
I only make your tides
and give some glow of light
reflected.
I do not shine of my own,
but in albedo-measured
mirroring
of hope.
For you are my sun and my earth.
mother of life.
and you hold me forever
in an orbit about you
so that you may look on
my face, forever waxing and waning,
period set by your
coming and going from my life.

the Eighty-Third Panther Cycle: the prices of love

RELEASING THE BUTTERFLIES

my hands open
and I release
the butterflies.
I thank them for
their gentle time,
but tell them the panther
is back in the
garden and I
must get to work rebuilding.
the picket fence
needs a new coat
of white paint and I smile.

53

OPUS 580:
THE BLACK LACE WINGS

I need your courage.
I need you to summon your nature
and grow the black lace wings
required to meet me.
Time and pain
have beat me down,
but I have yet wind enough
to fly
before I die
if the sky
is not hollow.
And I will swallow the sun
to hide your shame
if my name
is not good enough
to be carried
in your legend.
But I need your courage.
It is more than your turn
to follow.
It is your turn to carry.
If you wish my love,
pronounce it to the world
with joy and evocation.
For I give it simply,
and with joy.
Awakening the parson souls
of all the universe
who sigh in delight
at my every poetic kiss.

Amotations they wish
they had for themselves.
Meet me in the stars
and let us make a legend.
Or I shall make mine alone
that when I am gone
they may say...
there was a man
who knew love
and touched it
with bare hands.
A shame he never
felt it touching back.
But still,
it is good he loved.
Nonetheless.

55

LET ME BE YOUR HELPMEET

Let me be your helpmeet when the road goes on too long and the light
fades. I would die in your grace, so I would face the darkest night
with you. I will not turn an angry word or venomed thought against
you for, although I am mortal, my love is for you. Lauri, I danced
the nights away with only dreams of you and me, as it should be, exiled
for a season while wounds were licked and fantasies pricked that we
could live apart. But there is gain in my surrender, before the wild
and pitiless creatures at the gates of hell come for me to free
me of the sanity I would share with your for the rest of my days.
I promise you two arms to hold you, two hands to carry your dreams, one
heart to be shared with earnest faith, one soul to melt with in the
dream of an afterlife, and one mind to labour alongside you to make our
lives as rich and full and remarkable as mortals can hope for. All I ask
for task in return is your love. It is a great request, but I am a man
of great destiny, and I want my legacy to be one of hope and joy, not pain
and sorrow and loss. And you are the fulcrum of my history, there is no
mystery to that. You yourself revealed this elegant if terrifying truth
to me a long long season ago, when we were both in better shape to drape
our laurels on our legions of talents and march without hesitation to
the gates of tomorrow. I am here for you now. And will stand my oath
until the day I die, for there is no one, and nothing, I crave more of this
earth than that we be reunited in the love we have seen and felt between us.

the Eighty Ninth Panther Cycle: seven words

HONESTY

You didn't have to tell me all you told me.
But you did, and your little girl cringe
told me all I needed to know. Guilt like
silt washed down a river of self-deception
until you could not live with the sediment
blocking the harbors of your heart. Starting
for home. But not knowing the way there
because you cannot swear you've ever had
a place like home within your heart.

the Ninety Second Panther Cycle: the thunder
comes down

DEFENSELESS

dropping my guard, defenses hardened
in years of survivalism made irrelevant
when love arrives at the edge of my vision.
permission granted, dreams decanted to breathe
airs long forgotten. sultry stings, caught on
the ripstop nylon of a heart's windbreaker.
protecting me from the winds of sadness.
madness building to a crescendo. glissando
tears running like frightened children before
the boogeyman. aftermath of a lover's laugh
of sudden realization. no hesitation. no time
to waste to taste the heavenly fruit at apogee.
and we will find a way, bind a way to blind
a playful poet reborn in the morn of no more
mourning. so that I may love forever.

57

I DARED TO DREAM OF NIGHT BLOOMING JASMINE

You rose early this morning and walked the familiar furrows in the carpet
to stand, as you do, every morning, and watch first light enter her room.
if I am awake, I hear you draw a deep breath, awestruck and marvelling
at the feelings that flood you as you see her sleep, like the promised angel
of a distant fantasy, dreaming of a fist full of wildflowers once given to you.
your smile blossomed then like the night blooming jasmine, stealing the wind
to take dreams into the sky to paint other people's destinies.
but none shall find a heaven half as Holy as I have found in your arms.

WEB SITE

To read more of William F. DeVault's poetry, visit his
web site:

http://www.earthlink.net/~wfdv